EAST of the SUN

— & —

WEST of the MOON

Retold and Illustrated by

L á s z l ó   G á l

A FIREFLY BOOK

BRIGHTON

Cataloguing in Publication Data
Gál, László
East of the sun & west of the moon
ISBN 1-895565-29-4
1. Fairy tales.   2. Folklore - Norway - Juvenile literature.   I. Title.
PS8563.A39E38 1993   j398.21   C93-094452-6
PZ8.G3Eas   1993
Designed by: László Gál & Stephen Kenny
Printed and bound in Hong Kong

A FIREFLY BOOK

Published in the United States by
Firefly Books (U.S.) Inc
P.O.Box 1338
Ellicott Station
Buffalo, New York
14205

To

Virginia, Kathy, Debbie,

and

The Canadian Children's Book Centre

nce upon a time, deep in a dark forest, there lived a poor woodcutter. He and his wife had so many children that their small cottage was hardly big enough. They were all pretty children, but the most beautiful was Ingrid, the youngest daughter.

One night the family gathered around the table for supper. Outside, a cold wind blew and rain beat on the walls of the little house, for winter was coming.

All of a sudden there was the sound of tapping on the window. Tap ... tap ... tap ... three times. The woodcutter took the candle and stepped outside into the dark to see what was causing the noise. There, a short distance away, stood a great white bear.

"Good evening to you, good man," said the white bear.

The woodcutter stared in surprise at this polite greeting, but after a moment he said, "How can you say it is good? Winter is just around the corner, with all its many hardships."

"I could make you rich. You would have no worries

about the winter or anything else," said the bear. "All you have to do is give me your youngest daughter."

The man looked at the bear even longer than before, and thought of the easy life, with no worries. Then he thought of his beautiful daughter.

"No!" He exclaimed. "I cannot do that!"

"Think about it," said the bear. "I will come back in seven days to see if you have a different answer." Then he vanished into the darkness.

Inside the cottage the whole family was waiting, wanting to know what had happened. So he told them about the bear's promise to make them rich if he could take Ingrid to live with him.

Everybody was horrified, all except for Ingrid. After thinking for a few moments, she said quietly that she would be willing to go with the bear if it would help the family. So it was that, seven days later, she was waiting with her belongings in a small bundle when the bear returned. She said a fond farewell to her family and got up on the bear's back, and they disappeared into the woods.

"Just hold tight to my shaggy coat and don't be afraid," said the bear in a kindly voice. There was something about him that made her feel totally safe, even though it was dark among the trees and there were strange noises.

They reached the other side of the forest, and off in the distance, at the top of a hill, Ingrid could see a magnificent castle. Its towers, its turrets, its drawbridge, and even its walls all glittered with gold.

Soon they arrived at the foot of the hill, and the bear tapped on a rock. Very slowly, the side of the hill opened, showing a long, lighted staircase leading up to the door of the castle.

Inside the palace there were hundreds of rooms, all shining with gold and silver. There were many tables spread with the most delicious foods. The bear gave Ingrid a silver bell, and said, "If you want anything, you need only ring this bell and you will be served at once."

She spent the rest of the evening exploring the rooms and tasting all the foods. Only late at night did she realize how tired she was.

She rang the bell, and at once a door opened. When she went through it, she found herself in a beautiful bed-chamber, with a bed made out of ivory and pillows and curtains of the most exquisite silk.

Ingrid put on the nightgown that was left for her. Then she blew out all the candles and went to bed. No sooner had she put her head on the pillow than the door opened and a mysterious man came into the room and lay down quietly beside her. When Ingrid saw that no harm was meant to her, she fell asleep, and, strangely, she dreamt of a handsome prince.

The next evening and every evening afterwards, when she put out all the candles and went to bed, the same thing happened, and the dreams that followed were also the same.

Days and weeks passed. Ingrid enjoyed the castle and had all that she could desire, and the bear was very kind, but still she felt lonely, so, when the bear finally asked why she was so quiet, she told him how much she longed to see her family, if only for a day or two.

"Well, it could be done," said the bear, "but you have to listen to me carefully, and you must do what I tell you; otherwise misfortune will fall upon both of us. Your mother will try to take you into her room and talk to you alone. Let her talk to you only when everybody is there to hear what is said."

The next day they set off to see Ingrid's family. They travelled for many miles, but finally, in the most beautiful valley Ingrid had ever seen, they came upon a grand house.

"This is the house where your family now lives," said the bear. "I will leave you here, but tomorrow I will come back to fetch you. Don't forget what I told you!" With these words he walked away.

Ingrid's whole family was overjoyed to see her. They all gathered around her and embraced her with love as they tried to put their feelings into words of gratitude. They showed her all through the house, and reminded her that everything that they now had was due to her goodness.

She described the palace with its rooms glittering with gold and precious stones, and told them that her life was good and that she had everything for which she wished.

At first her mother tried to talk to her alone, but Ingrid was able to avoid her questions. However, after dinner, when Ingrid was growing tired, her mother took her into another room, and, before she realized what she was doing, she had told her mother how, every night, as soon as she put out all the candles, a mysterious man entered her room and lay down beside her, leaving before sunrise, before she could see his face.

"Oh my child!" cried her mother. "It might be a troll who stays with you every night. But I will tell you how you can see his face. Take this candle with you. Hide it in your clothing. Then light it carefully while he is asleep, and look at him. But make sure that you don't drip any candle wax on him."

Ingrid took the candle from her mother and hid it, and when the bear came to fetch her, she said goodbye to her family and left.

They had gone only a short distance when the bear said quietly, "Your mother's advice would bring great misfortune to both of us. Please don't follow it." She promised that she wouldn't.

When they arrived home, Ingrid went straight to bed, and soon the man came in and lay down beside her. She waited until he was asleep. Then she lit the candle and leaned over so the glow of the flame shone on his face.

What she saw stopped her heart: there lay the prince she had seen so many times in her dreams. She was so happy that she felt she had to kiss him, but, as she leaned forward, the wax from the candle dripped on his shirt, waking him up.

"Why didn't you listen to me?" he cried. "If only you had followed my advice, in one year I could have been freed from my stepmother's curse. She is a troll who put me under a spell. I am a bear during the day and only between sunset and sunrise can I live like a man. Now I must marry her daughter, who is also an ugly troll. They live in a castle east of the sun and west of the moon."

"Can I come with you?" Ingrid asked.

"No, you can not," he answered.

"Then tell me how to get there. I will search for you."

"That will be nearly impossible," he said, "because their castle lies east of the sun and west of the moon and no roads lead to it."

Ingrid was very sad. She cried and cried, until finally she fell into a deep sleep, and when she woke up she found herself lying on wet grass under a grey sky. The castle and the prince had disappeared without a trace, and she was wearing her old clothes once again. But this time she didn't cry. Determined to find the prince, she started her long search for the castle east of the sun and west of the moon.

After walking for many days through gloomy woods, she came to a cottage. An old woman was spinning flax on a golden spinning wheel outside the door.

"Old mother, would you know the way to the castle where the prince lives with his stepmother east of the sun and west of the moon?" asked Ingrid.

"I know only that it is east of the sun and west of the moon, but maybe my neighbour knows more. Take my horse, and when you arrive, just pat him behind his left ear, and he will come back by himself. Take this golden spinning wheel; you will need it.

Ingrid took the spinning wheel, thanked the old woman, and climbed on the horse's back. After a long and weary ride through the woods, she came to a strange-looking tree that was standing in the middle of a large clearing. The trunk of the tree had a door and two windows in it, and in front of the door, a little old man was playing with a couple of golden apples.

"Good day, sir," said Ingrid, climbing down from the horse's back. "Would you know the way to the castle where the prince lives with his stepmother east of the sun and west of the moon?"

"There are no roads leading to that place. Since it lies east of the sun and west of the moon, only the winds can go that far," said the little man. "My neighbour might be able to help you. He knows all the Four Winds.

The East Wind, the West Wind, the South Wind, and the North Wind are all brothers. They fly all over the world. But you have to hurry. Borrow my reindeer. He will get you there faster. When you have arrived, just let him loose, and he will come back by himself. And take a golden apple; you will need it."

Ingrid thanked the little old man for his kindness and went on her way. The road now wound up between high mountain peaks, but the reindeer didn't seem to notice that the way was growing steep, and ran on without slowing. By the time the clouds were so close that Ingrid could touch them, she had arrived at a huge cave. At the entrance a giant was sitting on a large rock, playing a golden harp. As he stood up to greet her, his upper body disappeared into the clouds.

"Good day to you, big brother," said the girl. "Your neighbour said that you might be able to help me find the Four Winds, and they may know how to get to the castle where the prince lives with his stepmother east of the sun and west of the moon."

In order to see her, the giant had to sit down again, so that his head was not above the clouds. "I wish I could help you find the castle myself," he said, "but I know only that your prince will have to marry the troll princess if you do not hurry. You can borrow my elk, and he will take you to the home of the Four Winds, who know every corner of the world. They may indeed be able to show you the way to the castle. They may even be able to take you there. When you arrive at their home, let my elk loose; he will find his way back. And take this golden harp with you. You may find it useful.

She climbed on the back of the elk, thanked the giant, and continued her weary travels. After riding for many, many days, she came to the house of the Four Winds. It was standing on the top of the highest mountain and was carved out of the rock that formed its peak. Four gigantic gates faced east, west, south, and north. Wide steps, also carved into the rock, led up to these four gates.

At the bottom of the steps, Ingrid let the elk loose and started the long climb up the mountain.

The South Wind, who had just come back from a long flight, was sitting in the great hall, trying to catch his breath. His cloak was woven from thousands of flowers, and the whole room was filled with the sweet fragrances of the meadows and the forests of faraway lands.

"Good day to you, sir," Ingrid greeted him. "Could you tell me how to get to the castle that lies east of the sun and west of the moon?"

"I know about the place, but I have never flown that far. My brothers will return soon; they may know how to get there," said the South Wind.

Suddenly the room echoed with the sound of rushing air, and the three brothers flew into the hall. When they found out why Ingrid had come, they all agreed that this castle was so far away that nobody had ever reached it. Nobody except the North Wind.

"Yes," said he, "I flew there once. But afterwards, I was so tired that I had to stay in bed for days. "Please take me there," pleaded Ingrid, and she looked so unhappy that the North Wind finally agreed.

"We will leave very early," he said. "Now let's go to sleep. We will need all our strength tomorrow."

It was dark when they left the next morning. The moon was still above the horizon when the sun started to rise out of the darkness in the east. They flew with such speed that soon they reached the end of the world. Land and sea disappeared behind them, and Ingrid was sure she could touch all the stars in the sky. The sun and the moon seemed to grow larger and larger. Finally, between them, in the far distance, the castle came into view, standing on a gigantic rock which was supported in the dark emptiness by four giants. Like a huge shimmering curtain, the northern lights formed a wall around it.

"At the main gate of the castle there are always two trolls standing guard," said the North Wind. "Trolls are very stupid; when they look away, just walk through the gate. They will not notice you."

He put her down gently under the walls of the castle. "Go," he said. "Do what you have to do and come back when you are ready. I will wait for you."

Ingrid tiptoed up to the main gate, and when the two trolls looked away, she stole in between them. Then she discovered the window of the troll princess, and, sitting down beneath it, she started to spin with the golden spinning wheel. Soon the window opened, and the troll looked out.

"How much do you want for your spinning wheel?" she asked.

"It is not for sale for gold or money," said Ingrid.

"If it is not for sale for money or gold, what do you want in exchange for it?"

"If I can meet the prince who lives here and stay with him tonight, you can have the golden spinning wheel."

"Well, that can be arranged," said the troll. "Just wait there and I will call you when it is time."

Ingrid was overjoyed. But when she was finally shown into the prince's room, she found him in a deep sleep, and no matter how much she tried, she was not able to wake him. She spent the rest of the night shedding bitter tears, and at dawn, the ugly princess chased her out.

She was determined to talk to the prince, so, later that day, she again sat down under the window of the troll princess, and this time she stared to play with the golden apple. Before long, the troll princess looked out. She asked how she could buy the golden apple, and they struck the same bargain as they had the day before.

However, when Ingrid went to see her prince, she again found him sleeping, and could not wake him up. This time, she realized that he had been given a sleeping potion. Under the cover of darkness, she hurried back to the place where the North Wind was waiting for her and told him what had happened.

"Very well," he said. "Just go back to the castle and make the same agreement. Don't worry. I will look after the rest."

So, at dawn, Ingrid went back to the castle and found a shelter where she could close her eyes and sleep for a short while. At the same time, the North Wind flew into the castle and entered the room where the prince was just waking up.

"Who are you? What do you want?" asked the prince.

"I am here to warn you that last night and the night before the troll princess put sleeping potion in your drink to prevent you from seeing the girl you love. She was here beside you, but she couldn't wake you from your deep sleep. Tonight she will come again. You must be alert!"

So that day, Ingrid again sat under the window of the troll princess, and this time she was playing the golden harp. Sure enough, the troll soon stuck her head out and, after some bargaining, they made the same deal: Ingrid would give her the harp, if she was allowed to spend the night beside the prince.

This time, however, the prince was awake when Ingrid arrived, since he had poured the sleeping potion out the window. There was great rejoicing. "I am so very happy to see you," said the prince, "for tomorrow I am to marry the ugly troll princess, and you are the only woman in the world who can save me and set me free. Now that you are here, I have an idea.

"I will declare that the woman who is to be my wife has to be able to wash my shirt - the very one on which you dropped the spots of candle wax - for only the one who can wash it pure white is fit to be my bride. It is a magic shirt, and the one who has soiled it is the only one who can get rid of its stains. After they try and fail, I will ask you to wash it."

The next day, as he had planned, the prince said to the troll princess: "I want to see what my future wife can do. I have a white shirt that I want to wear for my wedding, but it is stained with candle wax. I have sworn never to take any bride other than the woman who can wash it pure white again. Do you agree to this test?"

Well, the ugly princess agreed. She called for a washtub and for soap, and began to wash the shirt, but the more she rubbed and scrubbed it, the dirtier it became. The old hag, her mother, tried to wash it too, but the spot grew bigger and spread over the entire shirt. Soon the whole pack of trolls was rubbing it and scrubbing it, but without success.

"Well I can see that none of you can get it clean," said the prince. "There is a young girl outside. Maybe she can do it."

So he called Ingrid in and asked her to wash the shirt. As soon as she began washing it, the shirt became white as white could be.

"Yes, you are the bride for me!" cried the prince.

Hearing this, the old hag flew into a terrible rage, and with her all the other trolls. Their bodies began to shake so badly that soon they all burst into huge billowing clouds of smoke, leaving behind only piles of grey dust.

Ingrid and the prince joined the North Wind outside the walls, and the three of them flew away, leaving behind the abandoned castle east of the sun and west of the moon.

After a long journey, they arrived once again at the palace where the prince and Ingrid had lived before. Magically, it was standing once again on the same spot, on top of the same hill, but now it was even more splendid than ever.

The whole castle was full of servants, and preparations for the wedding between Ingrid and the prince were already under way, directed by Ingrid's mother and her sisters. Her father and brothers were looking after the guests; everybody was invited from near and from far.

The old woman who had given Ingrid the spinning wheel, the little old man who had given her the golden apple, the giant who had given her the golden harp, and, of course, the Four Winds, all had special places at the wedding table. The festivities and the merrymaking were supposed to last for seven days, but on the seventh day nobody wanted to go home, so they kept on celebrating. Perhaps they still are.